Developing Reader titles are ideal for using their phonics knowledge and car with only a little help. Frequently repeated words help improve fluency and confidence.

Special features:

Short, simple sentences

Frequent repetition of main story words and phrases

Careful match between story and pictures

Large, clear type

Ladybird

Educational Consultant: James Clements
Autism Consultant: Child Autism UK
Cerebral Palsy Consultant: Pace
Book Banding Consultant: Kate Ruttle

LADYBIRD BOOKS
UK | USA | Canada | Ireland | Australia
India | New Zealand | South Africa

Ladybird Books is part of the Penguin Random House group of companies whose addresses can be found at global.penguinrandomhouse.com.

www.penguin.co.uk   www.puffin.co.uk   www.ladybird.co.uk

First published 2024
001

Written by Dr Christy Kirkpatrick
Text copyright © Ladybird Books Ltd, 2024
Illustrations by Fran and David Brylewski
Illustrations copyright © Ladybird Books Ltd, 2024

The moral right of the illustrator has been asserted

Printed in China

The authorized representative in the EEA is Penguin Random House Ireland, Morrison Chambers, 32 Nassau Street, Dublin D02 YH68

A CIP catalogue record for this book is available from the British Library

ISBN: 978-0-241-56396-0

All correspondence to:
Ladybird Books
Penguin Random House Children's
One Embassy Gardens, 8 Viaduct Gardens, London SW11 7BW

A Home for Bugs

Written by Dr Christy Kirkpatrick
Illustrated by Fran and David Brylewski

"It is Bug Day," said Miss Zebra.

"Great!" said Tao Meerkat.
"I like bugs."

"I like bugs, too," said Noah Panda.
"It will be a great day."

The class saw a meadow.
There was a worm in
the meadow.

"This is the worm's home," said Miss Zebra. "Worms live in the earth."

"Here we are," said Noah.

The class were in the meadow, and they were as small as bugs!

The worm and a beetle were here, too.

"Your home looks great," said Tao to the worm.

The earth shuddered suddenly. Everyone jumped! They saw a digger.

The digger dug up the earth in the meadow.

"Oh no! The meadow is our home!" said the beetle.

Suddenly, the beetle was gone.
She was in the digger!

The beetle jumped to the earth.

"Oh no! All our homes are gone!" she said. "The digger dug up all our homes."

The class looked at the digger.

The earth shuddered again.

"Do you know what to do?" Noah asked the class.

"I know what to do!" said Tao.
"I have an idea."

"We can all help make a big, new house for the bugs," said Tao.

"Great idea, Tao! It can be a safe house for all the bugs in the meadow," said Noah.

"We will help to make a safe bug house for everyone to live in," said some ants.

The small ants helped to make the house.

Everyone dug up the earth and helped make the new house.

"Here is your new home!" said Noah.

"We have a home again!" said the beetle. "We have a big, safe new home for everyone. We like this house."

Tao and Noah looked in the house.

"It is great here," said the worm.

"Did you like Bug Day?" asked Miss Zebra.

"It was great!" said Tao. "Can we help some bugs again?"

How much do you remember about the story of *A Home for Bugs*? Answer these questions and find out!

- Why did the bugs need a new home?

- What did Tao Meerkat suggest they do to help the bugs?

- Who helped to build the big bug house?

- Who was in the big bug house when Tao and Noah Panda looked inside?